To anyone who has ever turned fear into friendship—B. R.

Miriam!—L. D.

AUTHOR'S NOTE:
Every word in this book is made
from the following five letters:
a, b, e, r, and w.
These are the five letters that
make up the book's title:
BEWARE!

Published by Charlesbridge
85 Main Street
Watertown, MA 02472
(617) 926-0329
www.charlesbridge.com

Printed in China
(hc) 10 9 8 7 6 5 4 3 2 1

Illustrations painted in watercolor over pen and ink on handmade
    Twinrocker watercolor paper
Display type and text type set in Graphen by Maciej Wloczewski

Printed by 1010 Printing International Limited in Huizhou,
    Guangdong, China
Production supervision by Brian G. Walker
Designed by Joyce White

Names: Raczka, Bob, author. | Day, Larry, 1956– illustrator.
Title: Beware! / Bob Raczka ; illustrated by Larry Day.
Description: Watertown, MA : Charlesbridge, [2019] | Summary: "Using
words made up of only the five letters 'beware,' a little bear named
Abe and a bee named Bree, who have been warned about each other,
compete for the flowers in their meadow, but end up as friends willing
to put aside their differences and share"—Provided by publisher.
Identifiers: LCCN 2018037907 (print) | LCCN 2018041702 (ebook)
| ISBN 9781632898289 (ebook) | ISBN 9781632898296 (ebook pdf)
| ISBN 9781580896832 (reinforced for library use)
Subjects: LCSH: Bumblebees—Juvenile fiction. | Bears—Juvenile fiction. |
Sharing—Juvenile fiction. | Friendship—Juvenile fiction. | CYAC:
Bees—Fiction. | Bears—Fiction. | Sharing—Fiction. |
Friendship—Fiction. | LCGFT: Picture books.
Classification: LCC PZ7.R1056 (ebook) | LCC PZ7.R1056 Be 2019 (print) |
DDC
[E]—dc23
LC record available at https://lccn.loc.gov/2018037907

A wee bee, Bree.

A rare bear, Abe.

"Bree, beware a bear."

"Abe, beware a bee."

"A bear? Baaa!"

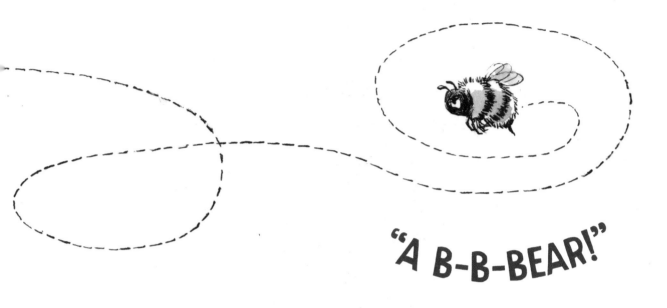

"A B-B-BEAR!"

A bee-bear war.

A bee rear.

A bear rear.

A wee-bee rear.

A rare-bear rear.

A raw rare-bear rear.

Eww, a wee-bee rear.

"Bear?"

"Bree, are we . . . ?"

"We are, Abe."

Aww . . .